THIS WALKER BOOK BELONGS TO:

JAMES RICHARD MORGAN.

5, CHESTERTON CLOSE,

CHESHAM,

BUCKS

For my Mother
C. Mc.

First published in 1982 by
Walker Books Ltd
87 Vauxhall Walk
London SE11 5HJ

This edition published 1990

Text © 1982 Russell Hoban
Illustrations © 1982 Colin McNaughton

Printed and bound in Italy by L.E.G.O., Vicenza

British Library Cataloguing in Publication Data
Hoban, Russell, *1925-*
The battle of Zormla.
I. Title   II. McNaughton, Colin
813'.54[J] PZ7
ISBN 0-7445-1728-1

THE BATTLE OF ZORMLA

Written by

Russell Hoban

Illustrated by

Colin McNaughton

WALKER BOOKS
LONDON

Everyone got an invitation but no one could read
the invitation.

"What does it say?" they asked the Empress of
Zurm.

"It seems to be written in Zormlan," said the

Empress. "I think you're invited to something."

"What?" said everyone.

"The Battle of Zormla," said a voice.

"When?" said everyone.

"Thursday," said the voice.

Everyone said, "Where is Zormla?"
Zormla said, "Here I am. Is it Thursday?"
Everyone said, "No, it's only Tuesday."
Zormla said, "We must fight."

Zormla attacked from the air with blazing
clementines.
"Stop blazing with the clementines," said the
Empress of Zurm.

Zormla attacked from the sea with a laser
sponge.
"Stop lasering with the sponge," said the
Empress.

Zormla put a bag over its head, no one knew
what it was doing.
"Where will Zormla attack next?" they all said.

Zormla attacked at the earth's core, led by a picked squad of one-eyed teddy bears with marmalade.

"Look out!" said everyone. "Zormla's got marmalade!"

"This is going to be a sticky wicket," said the Empress of Zurm. "I call upon the Council of Elders to help in the defence of the earth's core."

Zormla grabbed the earth's core and ran off
with it.
"Feh!" said the Council of Elders. "Don't eat that
earth's core, it's been all over the floor."
Zormla put the earth's core into the marmalade.
"Look out!" said everyone. "He's going to eat it!"

"Seize him!" said the Empress of Zurm.

"We don't want to," said the Council of Elders.

"He's all sticky."

Zormla's teddy bears attacked the Empress.

The Empress activated a force field and caught
Zormla in it.

"What are you going to do with him?"
everyone said.

"I'm bringing in the anti-sticky squad," said the
Empress.

"Zormla is *all* sticky," said everyone as the
anti-sticky squad moved in.

But Zormla was too quick for them. By forced
marches he reached the border and occupied the
fortress of Wendi Husa.
"If we can't seize him we'll have to besiege him,"
said the Empress of Zurm.

"I call on the warlords of Troon."
The warlords all said, "Troon has no alliance
with Zurm."
The Empress said, "The sooner the Battle of
Zormla is over the sooner I can make pizza."

"Okay," said the warlords of Troon. "We'll have
an alliance."
Quickly the warlords built a siege tower with a
battering ram in it, they were going to batter the
fortress of Wendi Husa. They were just going to

start battering when Zormla grabbed the ram and
the siege tower came down with a crash.

"This is getting us nowhere," said the warlords
of Troon. "We'd better send in some spies, maybe
they can find a weak spot."

The spies disguised themselves as paper bags and tried to slip quietly into the fortress of

Wendi Husa but Zormla tore off their disguises
and the spies were captured.

The spies put a message in a bottle and sent it to the Empress of Zurm. "Help!" said the message. "We are prisoners of Zormla in the fortress of Wendi Husa."

The Empress sent back a message: "Help is coming."

She leapt onto her imperial black horse and galloped to the rescue.

Zormla's one-eyed teddy bears made a sortie against the Empress, they were armed with heavy sticky. The Empress had to retreat.

Just then the spies found a dragon-class tank in their prison and out they rumbled.

Their mission: Get Zormla.

Zormla was heading for the scattered pieces of the Aarghian space ship. If he could put it together

in time he would blast off, he would escape the
warlords of Troon.
Pom! Pom! Pom! went the dragon-class tank.
Zom! Zom! Zom! went Zormla.

The Empress of Zurm was busy with the pizza.
"Hurry!" she said. "I'm putting it into the oven."
Zormla had the space ship all put together, he
was just going through his checklist for blastoff.
"Trimbles on!" he said. "Trimbles on," he
answered.
"Bimbles on!" he said. "Bimbles on," he
answered.

"Fullers on blast!" he said. "Fullers on blast,"
he answered.
"Blasters on full!" he said. "Blasters on full,"
he answered.
"Stop right there!" said the warlords of Troon as
they burst in through the airlock.
"Burst out!" said Zormla. "I'm blasting off!"

"Pizza's ready!" said the Empress of Zurm.

"We need three chairs here."

"Three chairs for pizza!" said Zormla and the

warlords of Troon as they quickly dismantled the space ship, sat down at the table, and ate up their pizza.

MORE WALKER PAPERBACKS
For You to Enjoy

THE HUNGRY THREE
by Russell Hoban/Colin McNaughton

There are now four books in this series – each as zany and zappy as the rest.
How many do you have?

The Great Fruit Gum Robbery	ISBN 0-7445-1210-7
They Came from Aargh!	ISBN 0-7445-1211-5
The Battle of Zormla	ISBN 0-7445-1728-1
The Flight of Bembel Rudzuk	ISBN 0-7445-1729-X

£2.99 each

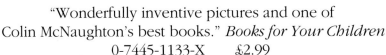

THE RAT RACE
by Colin McNaughton

"Wonderfully inventive pictures and one of
Colin McNaughton's best books." *Books for Your Children*
0-7445-1133-X   £2.99

THERE'S AN AWFUL LOT OF WEIRDOS
IN OUR NEIGHBOURHOOD
by Colin McNaughton

A book of silly verse and pictures.
"The book of the year for 7 to 10-year-olds." *The Daily Mail*
0-7445-1338-3   £4.99

**Walker Paperbacks are available from most booksellers, or by post from
Walker Books Ltd, PO Box 11, Falmouth, Cornwall TR10 9EN.**